Harriet P. Fowler

Vegetarianism

the radical cure for intemperance

Harriet P. Fowler

Vegetarianism
the radical cure for intemperance

ISBN/EAN: 9783337377601

Printed in Europe, USA, Canada, Australia, Japan

Cover: Foto ©Andreas Hilbeck / pixelio.de

More available books at **www.hansebooks.com**

VEGETARIANISM

THE

RADICAL CURE FOR INTEMPERANCE.

BY

HARRIET P. FOWLER.

"In a large acquaintance with vegetarians, we have never known one to be a lover of alcoholic drink or tobacco, and they suffer less from disease than flesh-eaters."—*Dr. Holbrook.*

NEW YORK:

M. L. HOLBROOK & CO.

1879.

TABLE OF CONTENTS.

CHAPTER III.

MEAT PERPETUATES INTEMPERANCE BY ITS STIMULATING EFFECTS UPON THE STOMACH.

CHAPTER IV.

TABLES SHOWING THAT OTHER ARTICLES OF FOOD ARE AS NUTRITIOUS AS MEAT, THEREBY REMOVING ONE OF THE DRUNKARD'S OBJECTIONS TO VEGETARIANISM.

CHAPTER V.

TABLES SHOWING THAT OTHER ARTICLES OF FOOD ARE AS NUTRITIOUS AS MEAT, THEREBY REMOVING ONE OF THE DRUNKARD'S OBJECTIONS TO VEGETARIANISM.
(*Concluded.*)

CHAPTER VI.

THE DRUNKARD'S SECOND OBJECTION TO VEGETARIANISM (THE SUFFERINGS OF THE PALATE) ANSWERED.

VEGETARIANISM

THE

RADICAL CURE FOR INTEMPERANCE.

CHAPTER I.

MEAT CAUSES INTEMPERANCE BY ITS ABSENCE OF CAR-BONACEOUS PROPERTIES.

IN the Appendix of "Fruit and Bread, a Scientific Diet," by Gustav Schlickeysen, translated from the German by M. L. Holbrook, M.D., editor of the "Herald of Health," we find the following paper : *

"More than twenty years ago I read in Liebig's 'Animal Chemistry' (translated by Gregory, page 97) how the use of cod-liver oil had a tendency to promote the disinclination for the use of wine, and how most people, according to Liebig, find that they can take wine with animal food, but not with farinaceous or amylaceous food. I was at that time a vegetarian, and felt in my own person the truth of this statement of Liebig, as also two members of my own fam-

---

* *A Cure for Intemperance.*—A Paper read by Mr. Charles O. Groom Napier F.G.S., Member of the Anthropological Institute, etc., etc., before sub-Section D (Physiology) of the British Association, at Bristol, England.

ily, one in old age and another in middle life. They had
for two years adopted the vegetarian diet, although brought
up in the moderate use of alcoholic liquors, for which,
after becoming vegetarians, they felt no inclination. I was
induced, by this seeming proof of the accuracy of Liebig's
theory, to endeavor to find whether it might not be valuable for the cure of intemperance. Having applied it successfully to twenty-seven cases, I will briefly give the results:

" 1. A military officer, 61 years old, of an aristocratic
Scottish family, had contracted habits of intemperate whisky
drinking while on service with his regiment in India, but
was well satisfied with himself, although a torment to his
wife and children. His habit was to eat scarcely any bread,
fat or vegetables. His breakfast was mostly salt fish and a
little bread. His dinner consisted of joint, and very little
else. He consumed during the day from a pint to a quart
of whisky, and was scarcely sober more than half his time.
His face and neck were very red. By my advice his wife
induced him to return to the oatmeal porridge breakfast on
which he had been brought up, and to adopt a dinner of
which boiled haricot beans or peas formed an important in-
gredient. He did not like this change at first, and com-
plained that he could not enjoy his whisky as much as formerly. About this time there was a great panic among
flesh-eaters in consequence of the cattle plague, and his
wife became so alarmed that the whole family was put on a
vegetarian diet. The husband grumbled very much at first,
but his taste for whisky entirely disappeared, and in nine

months from the time he commenced, and two months
from the time he became an entire vegetarian, he relin-
quished alcoholic liquors, and has not returned to either
flesh or alcohol since.

"2. An analytical chemist of some talent, but of intemperate habits, about 32 years of age, was desirous to be
cured of his vice. I called his attention to the statement
of Liebig. He said he feared that a vegetarian diet would
not suit his constitution, and that he felt that he had eaten
nothing unless he dined largely on flesh. I told him that
I had suffered from the same delusion myself, but I was
now convinced of its fallacy, and begged him to give the
vegetarian diet a fair trial. He was a bachelor, and had no
one to consult but himself, so, after several more objections had been answered, he consented to give it a month's
trial. He ate his first vegetarian dinner—which consisted
principally of maccaroni—with little appetite. Next day I
took him a long walk, which detained us three hours
beyond his usual dinner hour, so that he returned with
such a hearty appetite that he ate his maccaroni cold, being
too impatient to wait until it could be warmed. From that
day he persevered, aided by the diet, and before the end of
six weeks he was a total abstainer.

"3. A lady of independent means, about 42 years of
age, accustomed to live freely, eat very largely of meat,
drink a bottle of wine daily, besides beer and brandy, was
accused by her friends of being intemperate. Her sister,
who had great influence over her, took her, by my advice,

100 miles away from home, by the seaside, and after long walks they sat down regularly to a vegetarian dinner. In nine weeks her intemperance was so far cured as to be satisfied with about half a glass of brandy on going to bed, drinking nothing alcoholic during the day.

"4. A clergyman of habitually intemperate habits was induced to adopt vegetarianism, and was cured in about 12 months. He was about 44 years of age.

"5. A country gentleman, after 11 months of vegetarianism, was entirely cured of intemperance.

"6. A girl of nineteen, who, from association with intemperate people, had been led into this vice, was cured in about five weeks by vegetarian diet. After two years she went to visit those who had first misled her, and returned to a flesh diet and drunkenness. From this relapse she was cured a second time by vegetarianism. Unfortunately she returned again to a flesh diet and drunkenness, but was again cured a third time.

"7, 8, 9. A man, his wife and sister, all above 40, who had been addicted to intemperance for some years, were cured by vegetarianism within one year.

"10. A bed-ridden gentleman, slightly addicted to intemperance, was entirely cured by a vegetarian diet in 36 days.

"11. A captain in the merchant service was entirely cured of drunkenness in 44 days by the same means.

"12. A half-pay officer in the navy was cured of drunkenness by vegetarianism in about 90 days.

"13, 14. A clergyman and his wife, both addicted to intemperance, although of a secret and quiet kind, were cured—one in four months, the other in six months.

"15, 16, 17. Similar cases, all bachelors of intemperate habits, were cured within twelve months by a diet mainly farinaceous.

"18. A gentleman of 60, who had been addicted to intemperate habits for 35 years, his outbreaks averaging one a week. His constitution was so shattered that he had great difficulty in insuring his life. After an attack of delirium tremens which nearly ended fatally, two brothers, who had much influence over him, induced him to adopt a farinaceous diet, which cured him entirely in seven months. He was very thin at the beginning of the experiment, but at the end of the seven months had increased in weight 28 pounds, being then about the normal weight for a man of his height.

"19, 20. Two sisters, members of a family notorious for their intemperate habits. They were induced to adopt vegetarianism, and were cured in about a year.

"21. A clerk of great ability, who had lost several good situations on account of his intemperate habits, adopted vegetarianism as an experiment, and with such perfect success that one of his old employers took him back at a higher salary than he had ever received before.

"22. A governess, aged about 40, who lost a good situation on account of her drunkenness, was cured by a farinaceous diet in nine weeks.

"23, 24. Both military pensioners, aged respectively 56 and 63, who had contracted habits of intemperance in India. They led wretched lives on small pensions, until induced to adopt vegetarianism. They were cured in about six months.

"25, 26, 27. Three old sailors, above 50. They were cured by vegetarianism in about six months.

"From these 27 cases, in which the vegetarian system has been, within my knowledge, successful, I conclude that it is a very valuable remedy, and worth a trial. I will now give a list of articles of food which are pre-eminent in their antagonism to alcohol.

"1st. Maccaroni, which, when boiled and flavored with butter, is palatable and very substantial. I believe no person can be a drunkard who eats half a pound a day of maccaroni thus prepared.

"2d. Haricot beans and green dried peas and lentiles stand next. They should be soaked for 24 hours; well boiled with onions, celery, or other herbs, and plenty of butter or oil. Rice is useful, but less important than maccaroni or peas and beans. The various garden vegetables are helpful, but a diet mainly composed of them would not resist alcoholic drinking so effectually as one of maccaroni and farinaceous food.

"3d. Highly glutinous bread is of great use from this point of view. It should not be sour, for sour bread has the tendency to encourage alcoholic-drinking. Bread that is imperfectly fermented and liable to become sour is in very common use, and, in my opinion, greatly contributes to foster intemperance, as also the use of meat of the second or third quality. The use of salted food tends to promote intemperance, while regular hearty meals of fresh, wholesome, glutinous food tend to discourage it.

"I can speak from experience as having benefited in health greatly by adopting a vegetarian diet, and all whom I have induced to adopt it have been benefited likewise. It has the tendency to encourage the development of the intellect, to give increased capacity for mental labor, and to promote longevity and economy. The price of meat is double what it was twenty-five years ago, while the price of wheat, which varies, of course, with seasons, has not increased. Incomes and wages in general have risen, so that the poor man who is willing to live on wheaten products is better off than ever. He only feels the pressure when he attempts to live greatly on flesh, which induces a thirst for alcoholic liquors, for in all the cases of intemperance which I have examined, there is a special distaste for a farinaceous diet. Those who object to vegetarianism often complain of a want of appetite for such diet. Let such try seaside or mountain air, a good long walk fasting, or a ride on the top of an omnibus, and they will seldom want an appetite. The drunken mechanic, who, when sober, works hard, loses more time through drunkenness than he would in taking country walks, if such are advisable for his health.

"If we inquire the cause of a vegetarian being disinclined to alcoholic liquors, we find that the carbonaceous starch contained in the maccaroni, beans or oleaginous aliment, appear to render unnecessary, and consequently repulsive, carbon in an alcoholic form. Liebig says, 'alcohol and fat oil mutually impede the secretion of each other through the skin and lungs.' Nations living on a diet composed largely of starch, such as the rice-feeding populations of the tropical East, are less given to drunkenness than meat-eating populations. The meat-eating people of the north of France consume much alcohol per head—as much, if I may believe statistics, as the inhabitants of any part of Europe. The bread they consume is very generally raised with vinegar. One class of fermented food appears to attract another. I have observed that a taste for spicy condiments, butcher's meat and alcoholic liquors is associated, and that a taste for plain-flavored vegetables, fats and oils is likewise associated. I have known persons in the habit of taking alcoholic liquors daily, when eating butcher's meat, who find they must give them up entirely when living on a farinaceous diet without meat—their action, under those circumstances, being too irritating to be endured without great inconvenience—such as sleeplessness, burning in the hands and headache, and even nausea; and that in the same individual who, a few days before, with a meat diet, seemed to require several glasses of wine to prevent physical exhaustion.

"Lastly, were the ground now occupied in growing barley for malting purposes devoted to growing wheat or oats for bread and porridge, our national wealth would be greatly increased. But little wheat would need to be brought from foreign countries at a great expenditure of gold ; while intemperance itself, which is the chief cause of pauperism and crime, may be greatly discouraged by the cultivation of vegetarianism."

These results, obtained by the scientific testing of the theory of no less an authority than the great German chemist, Liebig, furnish certainly much valuable information, and, it seems to me, if rightly used, will prove of great benefit to the intemperate. But, as I desire to treat every subject in a fair and candid manner, I will say, for the benefit of those unacquainted with the fact, that for years there has been a great discussion going on among the savants concerning the destination of alcohol in the animal economy; and as this is the pivot on which the cure turns, let us consider the subject for a few moments. It was one of Liebig's propositions that it is consumed by oxydation, like any other non-nitrogenous principle. This view originally met with general acceptance. A reaction, however, was started by the discovery of MM. Lallemand, Perrin and Duroy (French chemists and physiologists) that alcohol passes off from the body in an unchanged state, after being ingested.

It would be highly interesting to cite the discoveries and experiments of all the authorities upon this subject, but they would fill a book ten times the size of this ; for there is hardly a chemist or physiologist of any note who has not "had a finger in the pie." To my mind, some of the strongest arguments in support of Liebig's proposition have been made by Dr. Dupre, but they are too lengthy to be here quoted. See "On the Elimination of Alcohol" (*Proc. Royal Society*, No. 131 and No. 133.)

To sum up the results of all the discoveries and experiments in one sentence: Although it has been proved that alcohol is eliminated from the system, it has not been proved that *as much* escapes as enters it. Consequently, we must believe that some of it remains, and is turned to account in the system. In verification of this, I will quote two of the many authorities at my command.

In "Marshall's Outlines of Physiology"—*one of the text-books used in Harvard Medical College*—we find the following : "Alcohol, which may be considered as one type of hydrocarbonaceous food, has been said by some to escape wholly unchanged, by the breath and the excretions ; but it is generally believed to be at least partly oxydized, either with or without previous conversion into aldehyde, acetic acid, or some other intermediate substance or substances. The quantities of alcohol found in the excretions do not appear to have been accurately compared by those observers, Lallemand, Perrin and Duroy, with the quantity actually taken into the stomach. Baudot and Thudicum have shown that when this is done the quantities eliminated are proportionally small. Even in the results obtained by Lallemand, Perrin and Duroy, only one-fourth of the alcohol taken is thus accounted for. (*Gingeot.*) In these cases, and also in those in which enormous quantities have been given in disease, more or less alcohol must therefore be appropriated, or assimilated, by the tissues, be retained in them, or be oxydized."

F. W. Pavy, M. D., F. R. S., one of the highest authorities in England, says, in "A Treatise on Food and Dietetics": "The position held by alcohol in an alimentary point of view has been discussed in a previous part of this work. It will there be seen that much divergence of opinion has prevailed upon the prime question, whether alcohol is to be regarded as possessing any alimentary value or not. It will suffice here to refer the reader to what has already been mentioned, and to state that the weight of evidence appears to be in favor of the affirmative. A small portion seems undoubtedly to escape from the body unconsumed, but there is reason to believe that the larger portion is retained, and turned to account in the system."

Chemically speaking, alcohol holds an intermediate position between the carbohydrates and the hydrocarbons. The former comprise starch, dextrine, sugar and gums, and their office is to support animal heat. They are also converted into fat, and of themselves have only about half the heat-producing and fat-supplying properties, as hydrocarbons, which include all oils and fats, whether animal or vegetable.

I am well aware that it is almost the universal custom of temperance lecturers and writers to assert that alcohol is not food, because it is eliminated as alcohol from the body. But they omit to mention the very important fact that *not all* is eliminated, which modifies their assertion very materially. I am a firm friend of temperance, and therefore regret exceedingly that this mutilated statement of the truth should be made. For, while it is naturally enough believed by non-investigating hearers and readers, there are some who are well posted upon the subject who see the blunder, and are thereby prejudiced against the good cause. For, concerning those who promulgate this error, they must believe one of two things—either the temperance advocates know better, and wilfully pervert the truth to carry their point, or they are ignorant of the subject upon which they are speaking and writing. I know that it is very exasperating to some temperance people to hear alcohol called a food, and, in some quarters, a person almost forfeits his reputation as a sound temperance man if he so commit himself. I think much of this feeling arises from ignorance on the part of the exasperated individuals, in regard to the exact meaning of the word food, as used by physiologists and chemists.

The temperance lecturer says to his audience : " How absurd to call alcohol a food ! Why, just compare it with milk ! Does it give us saline matter, as milk does ? No ! Then it cannot strengthen our nerves or build up our bones. Does it give us casein, like milk ? No ! Then it cannot feed our muscles or give us strength. Does it give us albumen ? No ! Or fibrine ? No ; it gives us none of these substances which go to build up the muscles, nerves or other active organs. Why, my friends, if a man should live on alcohol alone he would starve to death ! Yes, actually starve to death! Can we have any better proof than this that it is not a food?" [Immense applause.] And the audience is thoroughly convinced that everybody who calls alcohol a food is a great blockhead.

Now for the explanation. Any one food, in order to support life and health, must possess three properties, viz: nitrogenous, or muscle-feeding ; saline, or nerve and bone-feeding ; and carbonaceous, or fat and heat-producing.

Milk is the only food that possesses these three qualities in exactly the right proportion. Therefore milk is a perfect food, as we see in the case of the infant, every part of whose body is perfectly nourished by its sole use.

Oat meal and Graham meal and several other things possess these three properties in so nearly perfect proportions that alone they are able to maintain life and strength. Now, no physiologist or chemist, with any pretensions to scientific accuracy, asserts that alcohol is a *perfect* food like milk, or even like the cereals.

Liebig believed, and his followers believe, that it possesses only *one* of these properties, viz. : the carbonaceous one, and that it furnishes no saline matter, no albumen, no casein, no fibrine, and that, as the temperance lecturer said, if a man lived on alcohol alone, he would starve to death, in the same manner as he would upon starch, sugar or fat.

This experiment has been made upon animals, and they have always died. But when fed entirely upon the white of egg, which is pure albumen, and saline matter, they have died also, showing that starvation was caused, not by the one article being carbonaceous and the other one nitrogenous, but because neither of the foods possessed the three properties necessary to sustain life. The animals were geese, and if they had been fed upon Indian corn or oat meal or unbolted wheat, each of which possesses these three properties nearly in the right proportions, they would have lived and flourished. In dietetic parlance, *alcohol is a food, but an imperfect one.*

Mr. Lewes says: "In compliance with the custom of physiologists, we are forced to call alcohol food, and very efficient food too. If it be not food, then neither is sugar food, nor starch, nor any of those manifold substances employed by man which do not enter into the composition of his tissues." As a class, I have much respect for temperance lecturers and writers. The most of them are self-sacrificing, conscientious, noble men and women, and I am charitable enough to think that it is their over-zeal, coupled, perhaps, with more or less ignorance—or, let me use a softer word, misunderstanding of the facts in the case—that leads them to make such mutilated statements.

Mr. Lewes very justly and gracefully says : "So glaring are the evils of intemperance that we must always respect the motives of temperance societies, even when we most regret their exaggerations. They are fighting against a hideous vice, and we must the more regret when zeal for the cause leads them, as it generally leads partisans, to make sweeping charges which common sense is forced to reject."

The surest way to make sinners think the devil is white is to paint him a great deal blacker than he really is ; for sharp eyes will detect the undue coloring, and their owners will immediately begin to sing the song of the "under dog in the fight."

There is also another fact that must not be forgotten, viz. : that all alcoholic drinks are more or less saccharine. In some wines the quantity of sugar amounts to twenty per cent., or even more. In ales and beers the extractive matter consists principally of carbohydrates—in Scotch ale being ten per cent., Burton ale, fourteen per cent., which is the reason that such drinks are so fattening. Moreover, every drinker adds more or less sugar to his liquor, especially if he choose that which is not very sweet in itself. Indeed, the spectacle of a man drinking rum, gin, whisky or brandy without a liberal admixture of sugar, is about as rare as the proverbial "white black-bird."

Now, sugar contains forty-five per cent. of carbon, and as the theory has never been advanced that saccharine matter is not appropriated by the system, it follows that alcohol, as consumed by the intemperate—whether it be carbonaceous *per se*, or not—furnishes a considerable amount of carbon to the system. It makes no practical difference to Liebig's theory whether the drunkard gets his carbon from the fiery liquid itself, from the natural sweetness of the fermented grape or malted barley, or from the sugar-bowl.

If we look around among our intemperate friends, I think we shall find, as a general rule, that those who drink the

most liquor eat the least carbonaceous food, such as potatoes, white bread, puddings, etc., and the most meat.
Indeed, some drunkards eat but little except meat, and as
this, without it is very fat (of which few persons can eat
much) is almost destitute of carbonaceous properties, and
as the system must and will have such, from some quarter,
it follows that liquor is drunk to supply the requisite carbon.
Mr. Lewes, in "Physiology of Common Life," says (the
italics are his own): "Alcohol *replaces* a given amount of
ordinary food. Liebig tells us that, in temperance families,
where beer was withheld and money given in compensation,
it was soon found that the monthly consumption of bread
was so strikingly increased that the beer was twice paid for,
once in money and the second time in bread. He also re-
ports the experience of the landlord of the Hotel de Russie, at
Frankfort, during the Peace Congress. The members of this
Congress were mostly teetotalers, and a regular deficiency
was observed every day in certain dishes, especially farinaceous dishes, puddings, etc. So unheard-of a deficiency, in
an establishment where for years the amount of dishes for a
given number of persons had so well been known, excited
the landlord's astonishment. It was found that men made
up in pudding what they neglected in wine. Every one
knows how little the drunkard eats. To him alcohol replaces a given amount of food."

Mr. George Henry Lewes, whom I have quoted several
times, was the reputed husband of George Eliot, the famous
English novelist, author of "Adam Bede," "Middlemarch,"

"Daniel Deronda," and other works. Of the two Georges, George Henry, the husband, is less widely known in this country than George Eliot, the wife. But in England Mr. Lewes enjoyed a wide reputation as a scientific and literary gentleman. The "Physiology of Common Life," like all his other works, is exceedingly valuable and interesting. He has also written an excellent "Life of Goethe," "Seaside Studies," "A Biographical History of Philosophy," etc.

It is not presumed that any one with any pretensions to sound reasoning faculties or good common sense will for a moment claim that the assertion that alcohol, as consumed by the intemperate, furnishes carbon to the system, is to be regarded as a plea for its general use. It is true that we need carbon, but how much better to take it from the vegetables and cereals, as God made them, than to subject them to fermentation and drink it in the form of whisky, gin, beer, ale, etc.

How much better to take our carbon from the saccharine fruits (peaches have thirteen per cent. of sugar, grapes thirteen, and apples eight) than to throw them into the wine-vat and cider-press, and drink it in the form of sweet wines or well-sugared brandy or cider.

Why? Because, in their natural state we get no bad effects, but only good. In their fermented state their good effects are more than counterbalanced by their bad. In the former case, the partaking thereof will make us stand erect in our manly and womanly strength and beauty, the noblest work of God. In the latter case, the partaking thereof will make us fall to the ground and roll into the gutter, a heap of flesh and blood, no better than a pig, and not half as good as a Newfoundland dog.

The evils of intemperance should be truthfully and vividly set before the young.   Let not the *rising* generation be a *falling* one!   There is no absolute safety for any one except in total abstinence.   Therefore, let the accursed thing alone. As a beverage, in all of its forms, it should be banished from our families and social circles.   As a medicine, physicians, as a rule, should not prescribe it—not because it is incapable of doing good, for it is sometimes beneficial, but there is so much danger of engendering intemperate habits, especially in chronic cases of illness, that it is the part of prudence to substitute other remedies.   Occasions may arise when doctors may be justified in using it, but I think it is prescribed much oftener than wisdom dictates or necessity requires.   It is surprising how fond some M. D.'s are of ordering "stimulants" for their patients.

CHAPTER II.

MEAT MAY LEAD TO INTEMPERANCE BY ITS STIMULATING EFFECT UPON THE NERVOUS SYSTEM.

HERE are also two other reasons for the relinquishment of meat by the inebriate, and they seem to me amply sufficient to warrant vegetarianism, even were Liebig's theory cast to the four winds. It is always fine to have two "strings to one's bow," but how delightful to have three! The first we have discussed in the preceding chapter. The second is this: Meat, by its stimulating effect upon the nervous system, prepares the way for intemperance. That meat has this stimulating effect is shown by the following instances : In the "Lancet" (Vol. i, p. 186, 1869) we read : "A bear kept at the Anatomical Museum of Giessen showed a quiet, gentle nature as long as he was fed exclusively on bread, but a few days' feeding on meat made him vicious and even quite dangerous. That swine grow irascible by having flesh food given them, is well known, so much so, indeed, that they will then attack men." Those who have kept a watch-dog know that he is much more fierce, and liable to attack burglars if fed exclusively upon meat. In "Experimental Researches on the Food of Animals" (p: 24, London) Dr. Dundas Thomson quotes a narrative of the effects of a repast of meat on some native Indians, whose customary fare, as is usual among the tribe, had consisted only of vegetable food : "They dined most luxuriously, stuffing themselves as if they were never to eat again. After an hour or two, to his (the traveler's) great surprise and amusement, the expression of their countenances, their jabbering and gesticulations, showed clearly that the feast had produced the same effect as any intoxicating spirit or drug. The second treat was attended with the same result."

Again, when a man is stricken with paralysis (one of the most formidable of brain diseases) what does the wise physician say? "You must eat no meat. It is altogether too exciting to the brain." It is the best and almost the only thing that can be done for the sick man now, but it is like "locking the barn-door after the horse is stolen."

A few days since I was talking with a gentleman who has been a popular and successful temperance lecturer for over forty years, and he told me that long and careful observation had led him to declare emphatically that meat, by its stimulating effect upon the nervous system, prepares the way for intemperance; and that, other things being equal, the more meat people ate, the more likely they would be to become drunkards. When we consider that, during this long period of years, he had carefully noted the various causes of drunkenness in an immense number of persons in different classes of society, and in many parts of the country, we must admit that his opinion upon this subject should carry great weight with it. Other keen observers of the workings of alcohol—among them intelligent physicians —have told me the same.

"But how is this done?" First, it is a well-known fact that by its action upon the brain meat has an exciting effect upon *all* our passions. It is said that the actor Kean suited the kind of meat which he ate to the part he was about to play, and selected mutton for lovers, beef for murderers and pork for tyrants. Now, although the passion for strong drink would seem at first sight to be more artificial than natural, yet when we consider that seventy-five or a hundred years ago it was the universal custom for everybody to drink that wanted to, and that by the law of atavism we can inherit a taste for liquor from a grandparent or great-grandparent, even if our parents be teetotalers, it will be seen that, to many of us at least, the passion is more or less a natural one.

A Darwinian would probably trace this inherited appetite still further back. Brehm asserts that "the natives of Northeastern Africa catch the wild baboons by exposing vessels with strong beer, on which they are made drunk."

Secondly, those of us who are conversant with the different phases of intemperance know that persons of a lively, excitable, mercurial nature are more likely to have a desire for liquor than those of a dull, slow, stupid one. A man of a nervous temperament, as the doctors would call it, is more likely to drink than a man of a phlegmatic one. Having once fallen into intemperate habits, the former cannot become a moderate drinker, as the latter often does.

Now it follows that meat or any kind of food or drink, or any influences whatever that will stimulate the nervous system, will produce or increase that nervous excitability which is so favorable to drunkenness.

The veteran temperance lecturer, to whom I have already referred, said that he thought that the excitability of the nervous system which the children of drunkards must inherit, is as much, or more, conducive to liquor-drinking than the actual taste for it which they also inherit. An author, a lawyer or a clergyman who lives a sedentary life, who disobeys hygienic laws, who drinks strong tea and coffee, who eats a great deal of meat, who "burns the midnight oil," who gets insufficient sleep, who worries about his books, his clients or his people, is more likely to have drinking children, although he and a long line of ancestors have been strictly temperate persons, than a man who lives an active out-of-door life, who knows and obeys the laws of health, who uses no stimulating food or drink, who goes to bed early and gets up early, and who is anxious about nothing.

Many a mother—especially an expectant one —would consider it very wrong to habitually drink wine, lest her unborn child should become a drunkard. But she does not shrink from the excitement of balls and parties ; she does not refuse the indigestible, dyspepsia-causing, midnight

supper; she neglects out-of-door exercise ; she drinks
Hyson and Java ·strong enough to bear an egg ; she eats
meat two or three times a day; she weeps passionately over
the griefs and trials of Adolphus and Angelina, as portrayed
in a third-rate sensational novel—in short, she does everything to give her child a weak, defective, nervous organization ; and in this way, although the wine-cup, the brandy
and the beer-glass have never touched her lips, she gives her
child such a strong pre-disposition to intemperance that
there is much more than an even chance that it will become
a drunkard. This is a very important subject, and, comparatively, an unknown and unappreciated one.

There have recently appeared in the New York "Independent" articles upon "The Increase of Crime Among
the Young," by the Rev. J. M. Buckley, Brooklyn, L. I.
They are exceedingly interesting and instructive. Indeed,
the reverend gentleman handles this difficult and compli-
cated subject in a most masterly manner. He says : "The
offspring of those whose occupations are sedentary, who use
strong stimulants, live irregular and excited lives, turning
night into day, eat and drink very heartily late at night,
must inherit feeble, nervous systems, and an abnormal
strength and eccentricity of impulse. And this, wherever it
exists, must be fostered by city life. Meals, for children in
schools, are irregularly served. They have no appetite at
the right time, and eat ravenously at the wrong time. Boys
learn to smoke before they are twelve years old, and before
they are fifteen, instead of growing healthfully and being

satisfied with nutritious food, and having a perpetual flow of
animal spirits, they have an insatiable longing for stimulants of all kinds.   When the sons of parents that live un-
healthy, excited lives, but never drank alcohol (such sons
living in the manner described) show a strange propensity
to drink and to do bad things, the parents cannot understand
it, but the laws of nature are plain to any who will investi-
gate them."

We are a nervous, excitable people.   "Oh, well," says
an old fogy at my elbow, "this is one of the inevitable
thorns in our beautiful rose of civilization."   It is certainly
curious to·notice how the great majority of people like to
be "set up" by something.   No matter whether the exhilaration come from strong tea or coffee, alcohol, opium,
hasheesh (Indian hemp) or what not, it is very agreeable to
the most of us.   Aside from its bearing upon intemperance,
it should not be indulged in.   "But what harm does it
do?"   After undue exhilaration has passed away, comes a
terrible depression, from which the person is only relieved
by exhilarating himself again.   This is inevitable.   As
there can be no mountain in a landscape without a valley,
so there can be no undue exhilaration without a depression
of the nervous system ; and the higher the mountain the
deeper the valley.   This constant alternation of being on
the mount of bliss and in the depths of misery brings too
great a strain upon the nerves, and they cannot fail to be
injured by it.   For this reason I should not advise drunkards to substitute strong tea or coffee for liquor, as is some-

times done. It is possible for some persons to drink both of these beverages without injury, if used in great moderation. But I forget—no tea or coffee lover ever does drink them strong, *i. e.*, strong enough to hurt him. No smoker ever smokes very much, *i. e.*, not enough to injure his health. No silly woman ever laces tight, *i. e.*, tight enough to make her sick.

> "O wad some pow'r the giftie gie us '
> *To see oursels as others see us !*
> It wad frae monie a blunder free us
> And foolish notion."

But it is pretty safe to say that a drunkard, if he substitute tea or coffee for liquor, will take them very strong indeed; for his nervous system, accustomed to the much stronger stimulus of alcohol, will imperatively demand it. In all probability he will become a tea-drunkard—as much a slave to the tea-pot as he was formerly to the bottle.

It is a comparatively well-recognized fact that strong tea and coffee—especially when drunk by persons of susceptible nervous organization—have an injurious effect upon the nerves ; but the equally true and important one that meat has a like effect, is not fully appreciated by the great meat-eating public. Aside from its bearings upon intemperance, it should not be eaten so freely, and by all classes of people, as it is ; for it is provocative of many ailments and diseases, especially among brain-workers. In persons of weakened or naturally susceptible nervous organizations, its use is very apt to cause insomnia (sleeplessness) ; and meat may

lead to intemperance in the following manner : A man cannot sleep o' nights. He goes to his physician for relief.
The medicine-man says : "Take some lager beer for a
night-cap, and, my word for it, you won't know anything
till morning." He does as he is ordered, sleeps well, and
likes the beer so much that he takes it every night. In this
way he gets a taste for liquor, and in a few weeks, or months,
by taking stronger alcoholic drinks, he becomes a drunkard.
I do not say that this will always be the consequence, for it
is possible for some men to take a moderate quantity of
beer, all their lives, and never become sots. But for all
persons there is danger that beer will be the beginning of
intemperance; and in those who have inherited this vice—
in those of very nervous temperaments and in reformed
drunkards — it is almost sure, by creating a desire for
stronger drinks, to bring on inebriety. The world is full of
sad illustrations of the truth of this statement.

In pure beer the percentage of alcohol is so small (from
two to eight per cent.) that unless a large quantity be taken,
its soporific effect is not owing to its action upon the brain,
for upon that organ it can have no appreciable influence.
When the man loses consciousness, he has simply been put
to sleep by the hops, whose narcotic effects are more than
sufficient to counterbalance the exhilarating effect of the
small quantity of alcohol. Strong hop-tea would have answered the purpose equally well, and should always be used
instead of lager beer as a hypnotic.

I have been a great sufferer myself from insomnia, and

have often been advised to "keep myself well filled up with lager beer;" but I have always been afraid to venture even one inch upon the Devil's ground, lest he should get hold of me. Some physicians prescribe gin, whisky, rum or brandy in cases of sleeplessness. In these the percentage of alcohol is so great (in the first-named from thirty-eight to thirty-nine; in the second from forty-five to forty-six; in the third forty-eight and a half; in the fourth from fifty-three to fifty-four) that sleep is due to its action upon the brain.

There is no excuse for taking beer as a hypnotic, and I think the cases are very exceptional in which a physician is justified in prescribing the stronger alcoholic drinks; for the danger of engendering intemperate habits is so great as to more than counterbalance the benefit which they doubtless often afford the sleepless. Sedative and narcotic drugs should be administered, or it is far better, before resorting to medicine, to carefully inquire into the patient's habits of life, to ascertain if something is not wrong there. One of the least suspected causes is sometimes the excessive use of meat. There are numerous other methods used to produce sleep, but they do not come within the province of this work. Often a light meal makes an excellent night-cap. For a long time I have been in the habit of taking a cup of chocolate, made with clear milk, and a piece of bread or a biscuit, the very last thing at night, with the effect of causing sound, restful sleep. If I omit it, I lie awake nearly all night. One of our most distinguished poets, in conversation with me last week, said that he had been a sufferer all his life from insomnia, but had obtained relief from this distressing malady by eating just before retiring. The late Rev. Charles Kingsley, who had successfully tried the same plan himself, recommended it to him. The September number of the "Journal of Chemistry" says that in the New York State Inebriate Asylum a glass of milk is frequently administered at bed-time to produce sleep, with satisfactory results, and adds : "It has been recently stated in the medical journals that lactic acid has the effect of promoting sleep, by acting as a sedative. As this acid may be produced in the alimentary canal after the ingestion of milk, can this be an explanation of the action of milk upon the nervous system when it is 'shaky' after a long-continued use of alcoholic drink?" It is possible ; but it may also be explained in this way : the stomach of the drunkard, as will be seen in the next chapter, is always more or less irritated. Milk has a very soothing effect upon any inflamed mucous membrane.

If the mouth be sore, hold milk in it, and what a relief is felt. Apply milk to the sore stomach, and the result is the same. As there is nothing more prolific of nervousness, and consequent insomnia, than an irritable stomach, it follows that whatever will soothe the mucous membrane of that organ will be productive of sleep. I have known persons suffering from chronic gastritis (inflammation of the stomach) to obtain sleep from drinking half a cup of cream at bed-time, when other remedies had failed. I have obtained many a good night's rest myself from eating half an ounce of cocoa-butter the last thing at night.

But for persons who are not drunkards, or for those who have good stomachs, that do not particularly need the soothing effect of the milk, a small quantity of any digestible food, eaten at bed-time, will answer nearly as well as milk. There is something soothing, however, to the nervous system in chocolate, *per se;* and as milk, by the great majority of persons, is more easily digested than other food—and as the easy digestibility of the night-cap is a *sine qua non* of its hypnotic properties—it follows that chocolate made with clear milk is the best thing for a sleepless person to take. There is another reason why eating at bed-time should produce sleep. The presence of food in the stomach, and its digestion, calls more blood into that organ, thereby taking some from the brain, which places it in a favorable condition for sleep.

But this light repast must not be confounded with "late suppers," which would be likely to have a contrary effect. The third meal, whether it be dinner or tea, should not be as full as ordinary; for if it be, the stomach would have done its day's work, and ought to have rest until morning. Whether the person who sports the "gaunt, insomniac eyes" takes dinner or tea at six or seven o'clock P. M., he should eat only just enough to be moderately hungry at ten or eleven o'clock—a time when all honest people should be in bed. Then, after he is nicely settled for the night let his wife hand him the milk or chocolate, with a small piece of bread. After eating it, let him shut his eyes and tell her not to speak to him again, as she values her life, and in ten minutes he will probably be in the Land of Dreams.

CHAPTER III.

MEAT PERPETUATES INTEMPERANCE BY ITS STIMULAT-ING EFFECT UPON THE DISEASED STOMACH OF THE DRUNKARD.

THE third way in which vegetarianism cures intemperance is this: meat, by its irritating effect upon the mucous membrane of a diseased stomach, increases gastritis (inflammation of the stomach) which disease almost always exists in drunkards. By increasing gastritis, it increases thirst, its accompaniment. Thirst calls imperatively for liquor. Therefore meat perpetuates intemperance.

Commencing at the beginning of the preceding sentence, and verifying everything as I proceed, I will say that Austin Flint, M. D., whose "Practice of Medicine" is used in Harvard Medical College, says: "In chronic gastritis stimulating articles of food, such as meat and condiments, are not as well borne as bland aliments. Meat and stimulants are to be interdicted. The habitual free use of spirits begets a liability to it. It occurs especially among drunkards. Thirst is diagnostic, if habitual." Gastritis is caused in this way: pure beers and pure light wines would hardly cause it, because the percentage of alcohol is so small; but fortified or brandied wines, gin, whisky, rum and brandy (particularly the latter, which is so very strong of alcohol) by their burning effect upon the delicate lining of the stomach, irritate it and cause inflammation.

Watch a man after a debauch. When he has slept off his drunkenness and is coming to himself, he has a terrible headache, more or less nausea, and usually vomiting. He feels much as does a temperate man with a bad sick-headache. In both cases the men are suffering from an attack of sub-acute gastritis. The liquor-drinker takes soda-water, eats nothing for a few hours, and the sickness and headache pass away, for nature has strong recuperative powers. After the next debauch—particularly if it occur soon—the same sufferings follow, only they are of greater intensity and longer duration.

Subsequent indulgences still further aggravate the disease, until, sooner or later, it becomes chronic gastritis, and the stomach is more or less irritated all the time. Acute gastritis is a much rarer disease than the sub-acute and chronic varieties, and is very dangerous. Flint says he has known it to follow a debauch, and prove rapidly fatal, and that from autopsies he has made upon drunkards he thinks that some who have been supposed to die of delirium tremens have actually died of acute inflammation of the stomach. Thirst is an invariable accompaniment in well-marked cases.

I have never been a liquor-drinker myself, but from various causes, unnecessary to mention here, my stomach for several years was more or less inflamed, and I can testify to the terrible thirst of gastritis. Such a hot, dry, thirsty feeling always existed that I feel sure that, had I been a drinking person, it would, in common parlance, have "set me crazy" for strong drink. We all know that very salt food, or anything that causes thirst, provokes drinking. The German pretzels are made very salt, so that more lager beer may be drunk.

Now, every good physician, from whatever cause gastritis arises, prohibits the use of meat, as, from its stimulating effect upon the diseased mucous membrane of the stomach, it increases the irritation. For this reason I did not eat meat for several years. Meat cannot increase gastritis without increasing this terrible thirst; so how is it possible for meat not to perpetuate intemperance?

"But," says an ex-invalid at my elbow, "how is this? A year ago I had dyspepsia very badly, and the doctor told me to eat all the beef-steak I could, and to take brandy after every meal, which I did, and was cured; and now you say both these things are bad for gastritis."

I certainly do. But they are excellent for dyspepsia; for gastritis and dyspepsia are entirely different diseases, and require entirely different treatment. The latter is only a functional disease, while the former is an organic one. In the latter there is no inflammation, as in the former; but, on the contrary, the stomach is in a sluggish, inactive state, and needs stimulating to make it digest food. Therefore meat, from its stimulating nature, is better digested than bland aliments.

For the same reason alcohol is beneficial ; but there is so much danger of its causing intemperance that, as a rule, other remedies should be substituted. Dyspepsia often furnishes a fine excuse for tippling. Query : Should we have so many dyspeptics if liquor were not so often prescribed?

Another way by which meat increases gastritis, and therefore intemperance, is by giving the diseased stomach much more work to do than would vegetable food. For meat is digested almost entirely in the stomach, while milk, eggs and vegetable food—especially the starchy part—is digested mostly in the intestines.

I have heard people say : " I know that meat is more sustaining because I *feel* that it is more so." It is true that, apparently, it forms a greater stay to the stomach ; but this arises from that organ constituting the seat of its digestion, and a longer time being occupied before it passes on, and leaves it in an empty condition. But this does not prove that meat nourishes and sustains the system in any greater degree than other food.

It should be borne in mind that our physical condition has a powerful influence upon our mental and moral faculties, for good or evil. It is decidedly for evil when our bodies are afflicted with certain diseases. One of these is gastritis ; for there exists a strong sympathy between the stomach and the brain. The case of the poet Cowper fully illustrates this point. Afflicted with this disease, he suffered for years from excessive mental depression. He writes: "I awake like a toad out of Acheron, covered with the ooze and slime of melancholy." No one can doubt that the author of the "Olney Hymns" was a sincere Christian; yet while his stomach was in that diseased condition, he lost his religious hope and spiritual enjoyment, and thought he was under the severest displeasure of God. But, in the language of his biographer, "the medical skill of Dr. Cotton gradually succeeded in removing the indescribable load of religious despondency, and his ideas of religion were changed from the gloom of terror and despair to the brightness of inward joy and peace." Many physicians, and every specialist, in this class of diseases, have had patients who have been made mental and moral wrecks by its ravages — in some cases, the power of decision being so weakened that the person is incapable of settling the most simple questions of every-day life; in others the exertion of will power being so difficult that the energy, the vim, the ambition seem almost lost.

When we consider that every confirmed drunkard suffers more or less from gastritis, and that, in addition to this, the effect of alcohol upon the brain is so marked as to greatly interfere with its normal functions, can we wonder that moral and religious influences are so often powerless to save, or indeed permanently benefit, the intemperate?

The great desideratum has always been to find something that *will take away the appetite for strong drink.* The best minds in the country, and the most pious and intelligent specialists in the temperance cause, deplore the inefficiency of the means just mentioned. The Rev. Theo. L. Cuyler, D. D., speaks thus strongly in the "Evangelist," on the question whether conversion can be expected to take away the appetite for intoxicants : "In some specific cases there *may* be a total extinction of this physical craving for stimulants. But what Mr. Gough affirms, and what I affirm (from my long observation of the phenomena of drunkenness) is that, with the *great majority* of reformed inebriates, the ·appetite is simply overmastered, but not *removed.* It often lies dormant for months, and then breaks out like a concealed tiger from the jungles. Mr. Gough furthermore told me that several inebriates, who had loudly proclaimed that 'conversion had .extinguished their appetite,' have gone back to their old debaucheries. A friend of mine often told us in my church prayer-meeting that 'the grace of Jesus Christ had taken away his appetite for drink entirely.' That poor man, after two years of Christian sobriety, went back to his cups, and died last year of delirium tremens. I could multiply these painful examples by the score."

The Rev. George Leon Walker, D. D., has written two very able and interesting articles in the Boston "Congregationalist" upon "Sanctification at a Jump." Concerning the doctrine that regeneration removes the physical appetite for strong drink, he says : "Nothing could be more dangerous or untrue. Conversion does not always, if indeed permanently ever, remove an appetite for strong drink. The history of John Vine Hall, and of scores and hundreds of less-known Christians, shows that the physical appetite may remain often strong and well-nigh masterful, in many a man whom it would be the height of uncharitableness to call unconverted.

And this doctrine of complete eradication of appetite by conversion, besides being untrue, is also, under the disguise of cheer, a doctrine of profound discouragement. Many a true Christian, struggling with his appetite, may well say, if these calculations are correct: "Alas! where is my conversion? I cannot be a converted man."

"But is not God omnipotent?" I hear some devout soul ask. To a certain extent, and in a certain sense, He is; but it is also true that He is governed by fixed laws, which He is too consistent to break. For instance, when a man is in a confirmed consumption, God will not cure him. Sooner or later he will die, although hosts of pious and praying friends implore Divine interference.

Years ago, when good people saw their loved ones afflicted with scarlet and typhoid fevers, they prayed earnestly for their recovery, and when they died, it was considered a "dispensation of Providence." But now it is known that they are "filth diseases," and pater familias at work with his shovel in the back yard is a more effective agent than pater familias praying upon his knees in the closet. If there be communication between a man's cess-pool and his well, God will not avert sickness from his family, even though a hundred saints pray to Him to do so. In the language of Dr. Hodge, of Princeton, "the drunkard's appetite for drink is often a disease, a mania, that God's grace does not reach, any more than it does a fever or a fit of insanity." *This is the reason why conversion so often fails to reform the drunkard.* As in every other disease, the causes must be removed before recovery can be hoped for.

The drunkard's stomach and other diseased organs must not only be cured, but a vegetarian diet be insisted upon. Then we may consistently pray that God may bless the means used for his reformation. I do not deny that sometimes, in slight cases of intemperance, and, much more rarely, in those of longer continuance, conversion does appear to remove the appetite for liquor; for truthful men have testified thereto. But many of these are only examples of the "expulsive power of a new emotion, for awhile casting out an old one."

Moreover, in these cases drunkenness has not reached the state of being a physical disease; for when it has advanced to such an extent that the stomach and brain are thoroughly diseased, how can moral and religious influences take away a man's craving for strong drink? Neither will the grace of God enable him to successfully resist this appetite; for in these cases the will power is greatly diminished, or even lost entirely. But, in less desperate cases, in which a man is in possession of his mental faculties, Divine aid is the most effectual means, at present known, to enable him to *keep in subjection* his appetite, which is, however, a very different thing from *removing* that appetite.

In a great majority of reformed drunkards, the appetite is

as strong as ever, and is kept in check only by will force—sometimes, but not always, aided by conversion. "Well, if so many men can control their appetites, and can keep from getting drunk, why is not that sufficient? Why not let well enough alone, and not lug in vegetarianism?" I reply, I should prefer a more radical cure, for three reasons.

First, the man's appetite, in the majority of cases, not being removed, there is always danger of his returning to his cups again.

Secondly, the struggle between principle and appetite is so constant and terrible, and such incessant care and watchfulness must be exercised to keep from falling, that they are, more or less, unfitted for the ordinary duties of life. I know men who might be shining lights in the world, and who might be a great power for good to others, if they were not obliged to spend so much of their time and strength in keeping the serpent of intemperance under their feet. They are looking down, and watching the writhings of the horrid monster, while they might be looking up at the angels !

Thirdly, in some cases the mental sufferings of themselves and their friends are so great as to render their lives miserable. I know families of reformed drunkards, who are living, as they express it, at the base of a volcano, not knowing the hour, or the day, when an eruption may occur. It may never come, for, although the appetite is raging within them as strong as ever, they are men of tremendous will power, and they say they have it under perfect control.

We all know what this means. We all know that such a man is liable, at any time, to return to his cups. And this fear—this constant dread of the terrible calamity—takes away from his wife and children much of the comfort and happiness of life. Oh! for something to remove the appetite for strong drink.

But says a Vibbert or a Dow : "What's the use of talking about a man's *appetite* for liquor? No matter about that, one way or the other. Let the law raise her strong right arm, and let every dram-shop and rum-hole in the country be shut. Of course if men cannot get anything to drink, they must keep sober, however strong may be their appetite, and in this way this question will be settled, and we shall be a true temperance nation."

In the Boston "Journal of Chemistry" for January, 1878, we find the following :

"OPIUM IN MAINE.—The Brunswick (Me.) 'Telegraph' says : 'Every intelligent reader knows that the use of opium has increased enormously in this State within a few years, the direct result, without doubt, of the enforcement of the liquor law in many of the larger towns and cities. We learn, upon good authority, that one of the largest firms of manufacturing chemists in the country says that more morphine is sold in Maine, in proportion to its population, than in any other State of the Union.'"

If this statement be true, it is certainly a very startling

and lamentable state of affairs. I have no way to test its accuracy; but as the "Journal of Chemistry" is a very reliable paper, and as the same thing has appeared in other periodicals—and, moreover, as it is just what might have been expected—we are justified perhaps in believing it to be substantially correct.

I have already spoken of the fondness that most people have for exhilaration, from whatever source it may come; and if a drunkard's liquor supply were cut off, and his appetite not removed, I think there would be more than an even chance that he would resort to other stimulants. Now, the opium habit is not as bad for the community as drunkenness; but, as it is nearly, or quite, as disastrous to the individual, it follows that if all the drunkards in the country should exchange their liquor for opium, it would not, I grant, be "jumping from the frying-pan into the fire," but certainly from the fire into the frying-pan.

If a rigid Prohibition Law be enforced in our several States, and the drunkard's appetite for strong drink still remain, it seems to me there would be great danger that, instead of being a nation of temperance people, we should be a nation of opium drunkards. Some persons, who have friends who are trying to reform, often unwittingly place them in great peril by advising the use of opium for insomnia and nervousness incident to their drinking habits. Opium is a very fascinating drug, and should not be used when other medicines can be substituted for it. In view of the comparative inefficiency of all the means at present employed in this country for the cure of drunkenness—in view of the success of the dietetic treatment in England (and, may I add, in view also of the arguments I have endeavored to present?)—are we not justified in believing that vegetarianism holds out a larger share of encouragement to the inebriate than other methods?

CHAPTER IV.

TABLES SHOWING THAT OTHER ARTICLES OF FOOD ARE AS NUTRITIOUS AS MEAT, THEREBY REMOVING ONE OF THE DRUNKARD'S OBJECTIONS TO VEGETARIANISM.

T is highly probable that many who have followed me thus far will exclaim : "Well, it is a very beautiful theory, and it may be true ; but even if it be, I cannot become a vegetarian. How do you expect me to keep up my health and strength without meat? Why, I should be sick in a week without my beef steak and roast beef. Besides, I like it altogether too well to give it up. If you take away a fellow's liquor, you ought to leave him something to comfort himself with."

I have said before that, for several years, I was obliged to give up the use of meat, on account of ill health, and I can fully appreciate these feelings; for memory recalls the pangs that rent my own heart, and the vigorous resistance that I at first made when my physician vetoed the use of meat. Therefore, it is with deep sympathy and a tender fellow-feeling for those wedded to carnivorous habits, that I attempt to answer these objections to this new cure for intemperance. Upon the second objection I will speak in another place.

To the first I reply that if meat be removed from the bill of fare of most persons, the health and strength would suffer, for in many families it is almost the only really nutritious article of food. But there are good substitutes for meat, and if food *equally nutritious* can be eaten, then it follows that the health and strength can be maintained, and that food equally nutritious *can* be eaten, it is the business of this and the following chapter to prove. I purpose to give tables of the composition of meat and other foods, in order that their relative nutrition may be compared. I have a number of reliable dietetic authorities, but they differ very little in the composition of their tables. I will take them from "A Treatise on Food and Dietetics," by F. W. Pavy, M. D., F. R. S., one of the highest authorities in England upon this subject. Many of these analyses were made by Payen, an eminent French chemist. Although I have already touched upon the subject, I will further explain, for those unacquainted with the medical terms used in these tables, that by nitrogenous matter is meant that property that furnishes, in the highest degree, material for our muscles. By carbohydrates—sugar, gum, starch and carbonaceous matter—is meant that property that furnishes material for fat and heat. The same may be said of fatty matter, oil and butter; but starch furnishes forty-five per cent. of carbon; sugar and gum, forty-three per cent, and

4

fat, seventy-nine per cent. ; so that the same quantity of fatty matter furnishes much more carbon to the system than the same quantity of sugar, gum or starch.

This is a very important fact to be remembered, in our consideration of the different tables, as Liebig placed such great reliance upon the carbonaceous principle in food, to take the place of the carbon contained in the alcohol. By saline, mineral and phosphatic matter is meant that property that furnishes material for our bones and nerves.

Cellulose, which occurs in a few of our foods, constitutes the basis of the structure forming the walls of the cells, fibres and vessels of plants, and is of no alimentary value.

BEANS.

Composition of Haricots Blancs.—(Payen.)

Nitrogenous matter	25.5
Starch, etc.	55.7
Cellulose	2.9
Fatty matter	2.8
Mineral matter	3.2
Water	9.9
	100.0

Composition of Lean Beef.

Nitrogenous matter	19.3
Fat	3.6
Saline matter	5.1
Water	72.0
	100.0

Composition of Fat Beef.

Nitrogenous matter	14.8
Fat	29.8
Saline matter	4.4
Water	51.0
	100.0

Beans have always been a favorite article of food among vegetarians, and deservedly so, for they furnish one of the best substitutes for meat. It will be seen, by a comparison of the above tables, that beans contain nearly as much nourishment for bones and nerves as fat beef, one-third more food for the muscles than even lean beef, and nine times more material for fat and heat than lean beef, having, in fact, more carbon than even fat beef. To this carbon-aceous property is due the preference given them by Napier; for it will be noticed that they are among the articles "pre-eminent for their antagonism to alcohol." The bean takes its place among those few articles of food that do not sacrifice, so to speak, their nitrogenous to their carbonaceous qualities; for it is exceptional to find one and the same food so rich in both these properties. The experience of different nations, for many years, has proved their highly nutritious character. For hard manual labor they are fully as sustaining as meat, and by some considered even more so. They furnish a good substitute for meat for those who fast during lent, and it is probable, on this account, that haricot beans are so much more largely consumed in France and other Catholic countries than in England and America. Baked beans, which are so much eaten in New England, would not be properly classed as lenten food, on account of the pork invariably eaten with them. Among foreign vegetarians the haricot bean seems to be a great favorite. I have often been asked what they are, and whether we have them in this country. Curtis and Cobb, in their vegetable catalogue, dub the *Phaseolus Multiflorus* as the genuine haricot, having three varieties—the Painted Lady, the Scarlet Runner and the White Runner. The flowers and seeds of the latter are pure white, so that this variety is identical with the "*haricots blancs*" of Payen's table. The Scarlet Runner has a large, dark bean, and a gorgeous red blossom —fine for covering arbors and trellises. Vick says, when green it is the snap bean, *i. e.* the string bean of Old England. In his flower catalogue he gives four varieties. The Scarlet Runner I have cultivated in my own garden for several years entirely as an ornamental vine. Planted about the base of a long pole, upon which is perched a birdhouse, my eyes have feasted upon the column of luxuriant green foliage and scarlet blossoms, which seemed to support, with strong, uplifting arms, the home of the songsters.

Surely it combines in a most remarkable degree the useful with the ornamental ; for, during the summer months, the extreme beauty of its floral treasures ministers to our æsthetic tastes, while in autumn the fruitage makes glad that part of our being which delights in the pleasures of the palate. But while it is only in blossom, pray don't call it a bean-vine ! When a neighbor or friend—one of those delightful individuals who are always mistaking our swans for geese—comes into your garden, and, looking at your vine-covered arbor, says, "Quite a handsome flower, but it seems to me it has rather a beany look," and taking one of the leaves between his fingers, exclaims, "Yes, I declare, it is nothing but a bean-vine—only the flowers are red;" then assume a high and lofty air of injured innocence, and reply, "Bean-vine, indeed ! Why, it's the *Phaseolus Multiflorus*, a native of South America. There are three other varieties, one of them a green-house climber, and"——"Oh ! ah ! I beg your pardon ; I thought it couldn't be a bean-vine," etc.

Doubtless the other colored beans, so common with us, and the white, or pea-beans, do not differ essentially from the haricot, and consequently the remarks made upon the latter bean will apply with equal force to all beans. I think, however, as a general rule, that colored beans have more taste and character than white ones, which is probably the reason why they are usually preferred by vegetarians ; for it must be remembered that they do not put pork or beef with them, which render delicious the otherwise insipid white bean. But "every rose has its thorn," and as a drawback to their high nutritive value, it should be stated that they are somewhat difficult of digestion. However, when they are stewed and buttered, they are less likely to disagree with the stomach than when baked with pork. Canned lima beans are more easily digested than dried beans, but they are also less nutritious, as they are put up when green, be-

fore the vegetable casein, which constitutes their nitrogenous principle, is fully formed. The same may be said of
green peas.

PEAS.

Composition of Dried Peas.—(Payen.)

Nitrogenous matter	23.8
Starch, etc.	58.7
Cellulose	3.5
Fatty matter	2.1
Mineral matter	2.1
Water	8.3

From the above table it will be seen that peas possess the
same general properties as beans, although they are somewhat more carbonaceous and less nitrogenous.

They are one of the articles which Napier considers as
pre-eminent for their antagonism to alcohol, and the remarks I have made upon beans will apply with equal force
to them.

LENTILS.

Composition of Lentils.—(Payen).

Nitrogenous matter	25.2
Starch, etc.	56.0
Cellulose	2.4
Fatty matter	2.6
Mineral matter	2.3
Water	11.5
	100.0

From the foregoing tables it will be seen that the properties of lentils are almost identical with those of beans. They are very rarely used in this country as human food, and I give their analysis simply because they are one of the articles mentioned by Napier.

COCOA AND CHOCOLATE.

Composition of Cocoa.—(Payen).

Cocoa butter	48 to 50
Albumen, fibrin and other nitrogenous matter	21 to 20
Theobromin	4 to 2
Starch, with traces of sugar . . .	11 to 10
Cellulose	3 to 2
Coloring matter, aromatic essence	traces.
Mineral matter	3 to 4
Water	10 to 12
	100 100

From the above table it will be seen that cocoa compares favorably with meat, as regards material for bones and nerves; that it furnishes more material for muscle than lean beef, and nearly twice as much for fat and heat, as fat beef; so that it is not only an excellent substitute for meat, but, from its exceedingly carbonaceous quality, it seems to be remarkably adapted as food for the intemperate. E. Lankester, M. D., F. R. S., Superintendent of the Food Collection at South Kensington Museum, London, says, "In chocolate the albumen and gluten are in larger proportion than in bread or oats or barley. It is, in fact, a substitute for all other kinds of food, and when taken with some form of bread, little or nothing else need be added at a meal." Pavy and other high authorities express substantially the same opinion.

In tropical countries, of which the *Theobroma Cacao* is a native, its nutritive value is so fully appreciated that it is used by the inhabitants as a substitute for meat. Years ago Cortez declared that a man could take a day's journey on a cup of cocoa; but in this country it is thought by many to be "pretty much like tea and coffee, only it has a different taste." Such people will say, "Oh, I cannot drink chocolate ; it always gives me a dreadful headache." This would be the natural consequence if regarded as a beverage, like tea and coffee; for the same reason that a piece of meat, if eaten after, or in addition to, a full meal, would overload the stomach and cause headache.

These remarks apply only to cocoa, when ground sufficiently fine to be dissolved and the entire berry consumed by the drinker; but cracked cocoa, or any kind of cocoa that is so coarse as to leave a sediment in the pot, falls below this standard, as in the latter case it is only a decoction of the seed, and contains but a portion of its constituents. Chocolate, being the cocoa berry roasted, and reduced by grinding to a fine paste, is identical with cocoa, and is equally nutritious. Cocoa and chocolate have also another claim to the notice of the intemperate. They are sedative and quieting to the nervous system. I know that tea and coffee enjoy considerable reputation as substitutes for alcohol, some reformed drunkards, whenever they feel the appetite for liquor, resorting to copious draughts of strong coffee. Doubtless the stimulating effect upon the brain caused by coffee does take the place, so to speak, of alcohol; but this cannot fail to have an injurious effect upon their already weakened nervous system. To the shattered nerves of the inebriate cocoa and chocolate come with sweet peace and healing on their wings.

EGGS.

Composition of the White of an Egg.

Nitrogenous matter	20.4
Fatty matter	——
Saline matter	1.6
Water. '	78.0
	100.0

Composition of the Yolk of an Egg.

Nitrogenous matter	16.0
Fatty matter	30.7
Saline matter	1.3
Water	52.0
	100.0

It will be seen that the white of an egg is more nitrogenous than lean beef, and the yolk nearly as much so, while the latter is ten times as carbonaceous as lean beef, and more so than even fat beef. The egg is rather deficient in saline properties, unless we ate the shell. Nevertheless, it is strong food, and a good substitute for meat.   Dr. Edward Smith says: "It would not be possible to exaggerate the value of eggs as an article of food."

Dr. Holbrook says: "About one-third of the weight of an egg is solid nutriment.   This is more than can be said of meat.   There are no bones and tough pieces that must be laid aside.   Practically an egg is animal food, and yet there is none of the disagreeable work of the butcher necessary to obtain it."

CHAPTER V.

TABLES SHOWING THAT OTHER ARTICLES OF FOOD ARE AS NUTRITIOUS AS MEAT, THEREBY REMOVING ONE OF THE DRUNKARD'S OBJECTIONS TO VEGETARIANISM.

[CONTINUED.]

FROM the following table it will be seen that cheese has as much saline matter, and very much more nitrogenous matter, than lean beef, and that it has nearly as much carbonaceous matter as fat beef, showing that it is not only more nutritious than meat, but, from its great amount of carbon, it is particularly adapted to the intemperate. This last clause applies only to cheese made from the whole of the milk, as in this case the butter globules, which constitute the fatty part of the milk, are not excluded, as they are in skim-milk cheese, which is thus rendered far less carbonaceous, but more nitrogenous, as will be seen by the second table on the following page :

CHEESE.

Composition of Cheese.—(From Parkes.)

Nitrogenous matter	33.5
Fatty matter	24.3
Saline matter	5.4
Water	36.8
	100.0

Composition of Skim Cheese.—(From Letheby.)

Nitrogenous matter	44.8
Fatty matter	6.3
Saline matter	4.9
Water	44.0
	100.0

Skim-milk cheese is harder of digestion than unskimmed, and may be known by its close, hard texture, often requiring to be grated. The famous Dutch cheese belongs to this class. In speaking of this hard cheese Dr. Lankester says : "Of such are the Suffolk bang cheeses, made by frugal housewives of that county, who first take the butter and send it to market, and then make their cheese. It is said of it, in derision, that 'dogs bark at it, pigs grunt at it, but neither of them can bite it.' Bloomfield, in his 'Farmer's Boy,' sings enthusiastically of his native cheese, and adds this caution :

'The skimmer dread, whose ravages alone
Thus turns the mead's sweet nectar into stone.' ''

Our American cheese factories make it from the whole of
the milk, and therefore the ordinary soft, friable cheese of
our markets furnishes excellent food for the intemperate.
In this country, with our facilities for procuring meat,
cheese is used only as a condiment or relish ; but in many
parts of the Old World, where meat is not obtainable by
the poor, the peasantry eat cheese in large quantities, using
it as a substitute for meat, and from its analysis we see that
this is its proper rank among foods.

Dr. Holbrook, in "Eating for Strength," says : "One-
half of a pound of good cheese contains as much nitrogenous matter as a pound of the best meat." Dr. Lankester
says : "Where cheese is digested, there is nothing which contains so large a quantity of flesh-forming matter. Cheese
contains nearly twice the quantity of nutritive matter that
you get in cooked meat."

For laboring people, and those who take a great deal of
active exercise, cheese is an excellent substitute for meat ;
but the sedentary, especially if their stomachs be weak, will
find that, in large quantities, it is difficult of digestion.
The old notion that a small piece eaten after other food aids
its digestion is fully confirmed by Dr. Edward Smith,
Dr. Lankester and other eminent authorities. Shakspeare
makes Achilles say : "Why, my cheese, my digestion."

OAT MEAL.

Composition of Dried Oats.—(Payen.)

Nitrogenous matter	14.39
Starch	60.59
Dextrine, etc.	9.25
Fatty matter	5.50
Cellulose	7.02
Mineral matter	3.25
	100.00

From the above table it will be seen that oat meal furnishes as much material for muscle as fat beef; that the percentage of saline matter is high, and that it is 7 per cent. more carbonaceous than fat beef, showing that it is not only a good substitute for meat, but suitable food for the inebriate. Oat meal may be called the national dish of Scotland. According to Dr. Edward Smith, who carefully investigated this subject, the fine physical condition of the Scotch is, in a great part, the result of their diet of oat meal and milk. It is so rich in phosphorus that it is an excellent food for brain-workers. According to Dr. Holbrook, Gerald Massey swears by oat meal porridge as a brain-inspiring compound. "There is a deal of phosphorus in oat meal," Mr. Massey says, "and phosphorus is brain. There is also a large amount of phosphorus in fish. Consequently I never miss having a fish dinner at least once a week, and take a plate of good, thick, coarse, well-boiled oat meal every morning in my life."

In answer to the assertion that men cannot do hard work without meat, we need only mention Hugh Miller, the famous Scotch geologist, who labored for years as one of a gang of stone-masons, living entirely upon oat meal cake and oat meal mush, with occasionally a little milk, given them by the farmers.

Oat meal mush, about which there has been such a hue and cry of late, is very excellent, but spoon-victuals, by frequent repetition, grow wearisome. I do not really think God intended man to be a mush-eating animal, for I notice that all the people whom I see are furnished more or less with teeth ; therefore I would recommend oaten bread. This is made of oat-*flour*, which is oats ground as fine as Haxall flour, and should be used for bread, wafers and biscuit, instead of the oat-*meal* which is usually employed for this purpose. I never ate any oat meal productions that were not full of little kernels of the dried grain that had been rendered by baking as hard as particles of uncooked rice. This condition makes their digestion and assimilation an impossibility, passing through the alimentary canal unchanged, without nourishing the system at all. The ends also are so sharp that they are very liable to irritate the stomach and bowels, and even to stick into the intestines. The Scotch sometimes suffer from this painful and dangerous disease. Of course this difficulty is entirely obviated by using oat-*flour*. I wonder that this fine oaten flour is not generally eaten, for beside being exceedingly nutritious, it is really delicious, having a rich, nutty taste, that no bolted flour ever possesses.

FISH.

Pavy says : "Fish does not possess the satisfying and stimulating properties that belong to the flesh of quadrupeds and birds. Still, the health and vigor of the inhabitants of fishing towns, where fish may form the only kind of animal food consumed, show that it is capable of contributing in an effective manner to the maintenance of the body, under active conditions of life. On account of its being less satisfying than meat, the appetite returns at shorter intervals and a larger quantity is required."

As regards its carbonaceous qualities, a great diversity exists in fish. The flesh of the white fish, as the haddock and cod, contains but very little fat, the oil being accumulated in the liver, whence we obtain our cod-liver oil, whereas the mackerel, the salmon, the eel and some others are characterized by the presence of fatty matter, incorporated with the flesh. Fish might be a useful food for the intemperate on account of its phosphatic nature, which would tend to strengthen and build up their weakened nervous systems.

MACARONI.

Macaroni, Napier places first in the list of articles preeminent for their antagonism to alcohol, not only on account of its carbonaceous, but its glutinous character. He also recommends highly glutinous bread. Both bolted and unbolted wheat are glutinous, and to this property they owe their aptitude for being made into bread.

The Cold Air Attrition Whole Wheat Flour—sometimes

called the Cold Blast Flour—contains the whole of the wheat, although it is as fine as Haxall flour. If I mistake not, it claims to be the most glutinous of all flours, and as it is more nutritious than macaroni I should advise that the latter be not used to the exclusion of the former. It is one of the great mistakes of the age to bring up children on bolted flour, because nearly all the material or food for our bones and nerves resides in the dark portions of the grain, which is excluded by the bolting process, leaving little except the carbonaceous portion. If everybody should eat bread made from unbolted wheat, oats and Indian corn, to the utter exclusion of bolted flour, it would be a sad day for the two D.'s in our community—the doctors and the dentists.

It is the universal opinion among the most scientific of our tooth-pullers, that one great cause of the early decay of the teeth is the consumption of fine white flour, inasmuch as it is deficient in those saline properties which are their necessary constituents.

Tapioca, sago and other strictly farinaceous foods may be eaten by way of variety, but it must be borne in mind that although exceedingly carbonaceous, they are so very deficient in nitrogenous matter that were they used as sole articles of food we should soon lose our nervous and muscular strength. It is curious to notice how the instinct [shall we call it?] of different nations recognizes this fact. Rice, poor in nutriment, and beans, excessively nitrogenous, form the food of large populations in India.

The Italian makes a good meal of macaroni, deficient in

5

nitrogenous matter, and cheese, which contains an excess of that quality. This combination is eaten to some extent in this country, and unlike the plain macaroni, is very nutritious. This is a very old dish, dating back to the fourteenth century.

Composition of Indian Corn Meal.—(From Letheby).

Nitrogenous matter	11.1
Carbohydrates	65.1
Fatty matter	8.1
Saline matter	1.7
Water	14.0
	100.0

From the above table it will be seen that Indian corn meal is quite a remarkable food; for although it is exceedingly carbonaceous, having an equivalent of 81 per cent. of starch (rice has only 75 per cent.), it has still a fair share of nitrogenous matter, nearly twice as much as rice.

It is two-thirds as nitrogenous as fat beef, and much more carbonaceous, being necessarily the most fattening article of vegetable diet known, as every poultry-raiser and farmer will testify.

It is very suitable food for the inebriate, and may be eaten in a variety of forms—cakes, bread, mush, and baked and boiled puddings.

GARDEN VEGETABLES.

Napier does not place very much reliance upon them in the cure of intemperance, for with the exception of the potato, they are only slightly carbonaceous. This tuber is the only one that has more than one per cent. of nitrogenous matter, showing that they occupy a very low place in the scale of nutrition. But as they are pretty rich in saline properties, and as they are very enjoyable, they may be freely eaten, with more nutritious food.

Composition of the Potato.—(From Payen).

Nitrogenous matter	2.50
Starch	20.00
Cellulose	1.04
Sugar and gummy matter	1.09
Fatty matter	0.11
Pectates, citrates, phosphates and silicates of lime, magnesia, potash and soda	1.26
Water	74.00
	100.00

From the above table it will be seen that the potato, although poor in nitrogenous, is pretty rich in carbonaceous matter. It is well adapted to be eaten with eggs, cheese, beans, or any excessively nutritious articles of food.

FRUIT.

Fruit is a very agreeable and refreshing article of diet, but its proportion of nitrogenous matter is too low, and of water

too high, to allow it to possess much nutritive value. Dr.
Holbrook and Dr. Gustav Schlickeysen give the apple the pre-
eminence, as regards nutrition. When ripe, the most natural,
and therefore the best way, to eat fruit, is in the raw state, but
weak stomachs and bowels cannot always digest it. When
this is the case, their owners are apt to abstain from it altogether. This is wrong. Cook it, and thereby it is rendered
more digestible. Every one in the country should have a
flower and vegetable garden, and should work in it too. I
enjoy very much taking care of my own garden—*by proxy*.
Especially should our wives and daughters spend as much
of their time as possible out of doors. No garden is complete without a beautiful woman in it. So thought God,
thousands of years ago, and so has thought every sensible
person since.

For the benefit of those whose minds are not constructed
on tabular principles, and who may not have been sufficiently
convinced by the preceding analysis, I give the following cases
illustrative of the strength-giving properties of vegetable food.
The late Dr. Mussey says: "The porters at Smyrna are noted
for their strength. With the aid of the Turkish pack-saddle
they carry on their backs loads that to an American or Euro-
pean seem almost fabulous. Capt. Samuel Rea informed me
that he was one of a party who detained one of these porters
as he was passing the office of Mr. Offley, formerly our consul
at Smyrna, and weighed his load, which was of boards. It
amounted to nine hundred and five pounds! The usual load
for these men is a box of sugar, and with this on their backs

they will trudge all day from the ships to the ware-houses. And yet their diet is bread, water, figs and other fruits."

"The Hon. Mr. Buckingham assured me that he saw at Calcutta men from the Himalaya Mountains, who made exhibitions as athletæ, whose strength was nearly equal to that of *three* of the strongest Europeans picked from the regiments and ships then there. They could grasp a man, with one hand on his breast and the other on his back, and hold him in the air at 'arm's-length' so tightly that he could not escape. Yet these men never had used any drink stronger than water, nor did they eat animal food."

Many other instances are given by Dr. Mussey, but I will give only one more. Frederick Field, Esq., in a lecture on "The Mineral Treasures of the Andes,"* says: "In the year 1851 I begged Senor Ermeneta, the proprietor of some of the richest mines in Chili, to send some specimens for the great exhibition, as samples of Chilian wealth. He forwarded me two large stones, one weighing three hundred and fifty-six pounds, and the other three hundred and forty-nine pounds, and told me that perhaps the strength of the miner who excavated these masses, and brought them from the mine, was as striking as the richness of the specimens themselves. Both stones had been taken from a depth of more than three hundred feet, and had separately been borne on the shoulders of a man, he having to ascend, not by ladders or other aid, but by climbing up the nearly perpendicular slope of the mine ; and the food the miner lives upon is an interesting subject for

---

* Royal Institution, London, Feb. 3, 1860.

physiologists.   He seldom takes meat, and when he has that luxury it is simply served out in long thin strips, which have been dried in the sun.   His chief diet is the *haricot bean*, and without this nutritious vegetable he could never get through the work required of him.   The beans are boiled until they are quite soft, and are eaten with a little bread."

CHAPTER VI.

*THE DRUNKARD'S SECOND OBJECTION TO VEGETARIANISM
(THE SUFFERINGS OF THE PALATE) ANSWERED.*

TO the second objection, "I like meat altogether too well to give it up," etc., I reply, the desire for meat is greatly diminished if the system is well nourished by food equally nutritious. Also, the more varied and palatable the bill-of-fare, the less will be the longing for meat. There will be a great difference in different persons in regard to the hankering after meat, some appearing to be naturally more carnivorous than others. And candor compels me to say that although in many cases highly nutritious, varied and palatable food will remove in a great measure the desire for meat, still there will be some who will crave it, especially when brought into contact with it.

I have heard of some vegetarians saying, and this has been my experience, that they felt satisfied with their food, except when they saw or smelled meat, when a strong desire possessed them to eat it. If a man finds he cannot sit down at the table with his family with a dish of meat before him, without an irresistible desire to eat it with them, then it becomes their duty to give up eating meat also. "Wherefore if meat make my brother to offend, I will eat no flesh while the world standeth, lest I make my brother to offend," should be the language of their hearts. And let them rest assured that if equally nutritious food be eaten they will not suffer in health and strength from the deprivation.

With the system well nourished with suitable food, and all temptation removed by the banishment of meat from the family table, I think those cases will be exceptional where the relinquishment of meat will be attended with any serious suffering to the palate. Let those few individuals thank God, and Liebig, that their discomfort is no greater, for the desire for meat cannot be *as strong* as the desire for liquor, which they otherwise would have.

To those anxious mammas who will enquire, "Why, how can I bring up my family in any kind of health or strength without meat?" I answer, the healthiest children in the world have been raised without it. All of us have seen young Irish and Scotch girls, who have come to this country as servants, who have been almost perfect specimens of physical perfection, with their rounded forms, their full busts, their rosy cheeks, and their white teeth. They tell us that they have very rarely eaten meat, but their food has been oat meal, buttermilk, goats' milk, cabbage, potatoes, eggs and cheese.

They fall into our cake, pie, and hot-biscuit eating habits, and although they eat meat, in a few years they patronize the dentist, the doctor, and the apothecary nearly as much as do their mistresses. I have already spoken of unbolted wheat bread. Let children eat freely of this, of milk, of fruits and vegetables, and of all the substitutes for meat, which I have mentioned ; let them never drink tea or coffee ; and if their other hygienic habits are good they will grow up fully as healthy, if not more so, than those who are allowed to indulge their carnivorous tastes.

For young children, however, cheese and beans are not suitable, as they tax the digestive powers too heavily. It is particularly important that the children of drunkards should not eat meat, for inheriting, as they do, a tendency to their parents' vice, they are more liable than others to be excited by its use to drink liquor.

It will be noticed that I have advised the lax vegetarian diet. This I have done for three reasons :

First. Although it is not mentioned in Napier's cases whether the lax or the strict vegetarian system was used, it is evident, from his advising that vegetables be eaten with butter or oil, that they were conducted on the lax system, for the strict one prohibits the use of butter, classing it as an animal food.

"Stick to your text" is a good motto, and as Napier's paper is the text to our sermon, we must follow it.

Second. The strict vegetarian system prohibits milk. Now this we cannot spare from our drunkard's bill-of-fare ; for, as a general rule, in gastritis, it is better borne than other food, and in some cases it is the only food the stomach will tolerate.

Cream is also exceedingly soothing and grateful to the inflamed mucous membrane of the stomach. Taken when empty it has the same beneficial effect that it has on a sunburnt face or frost-bitten lips.

Third. As I have said before, the more varied and palatable the drunkard's bill-of-fare, the less will he feel the desire for meat. His stomach being weakened, and usually more or less diseased, his appetite is poor and capricious; and if cheese, eggs, fish, milk, cream and butter, and food prepared from them were taken from his *menu*, his table would be deprived of so many savory dishes that he would be very likely to return to the "flesh-pots of Egypt." Moreover, the two first-named articles are excellent substitutes for meat, and for that reason could poorly be spared from the drunkard's bill-of-fare. The "Fruit and Bread" diet of Gustav Schlick-eysen, about which Dr. Holbrook tells us, in his excellent translation of that work, is a very beautiful and admirable one in many respects; but it seems to me it is too great a jump to take at once. Between the present mixed diet of our people and that of the wise German let there be a broad stepping-stone—lax vegetarianism.

It is claimed that if the fruit and bread diet were used, woman would be emancipated from the drudgery of the kitchen. But *lax* vegetarianism would do this quite as effectually. For it is no more labor to milk a cow than it is to pick fruit. It is no more labor to skim milk than it is to hull strawberries. One can as easily boil an egg, or beat it raw, as crack a dish of nuts.

Butter-making can hardly be classed among the drudgeries

of the kitchen, for very few women, except farmers' wives, make butter. Moreover, let butter go to the four winds, and let us eat the fatty globules of milk, in the form of cream. Very few women in this country make cheese, the great bulk of it being furnished by our cheese-factories, where men and machinery are employed.

But there are three articles of food which do entail an immense expenditure of time and labor upon women, and they should be banished as far as possible (to Jericho, for example) from our families. These are pie, cake and white-flour biscuit. We are a pie-eating people, and to this cause we owe much of our national dyspepsia. Men, as a general rule, are more fond of it than women. I know of some who will have it three times a day. Says the wife of such an one : "What can I do? I'm all tired out making so many pies for John ; but he's very fond of them, and will have them. Now, do you think I ought to put my foot down and say I won't make them for him ?"

No, certainly not. You may set before him their un-healthful character; and the toil and trouble of making them. You may gently entreat and mildly coax him to give them up. You may even do the bewitching, as sweetly and faithfully as possible. By pursuing this course of treatment there is about an even chance that he will see the error of his ways. But if he turn a deaf ear to your arguments and a blind eye to your blandishments, and persist in wanting his pie, it is your duty to make it for him, without one sour look or one word of complaint. But you need not make any pie for yourself or children, and that will lessen your burden very materially. Of course the little folks will clamor for it, and will want to know why they cannot have pie, as well as papa. Then make them this little speech; "Children, pie is not good for your health, and it is not good for mine to make it for you. So you will have no more pie; for you are my children, and I have a perfect right to control you and make you obey me. Your father wishes me to make it for him, and I shall do so, for he is my husband, and it is my duty to please and obey him."

Say this and stick to it. Ten to one John will say : " Yes, children, your mother is right, and you must mind what she says. Pie is very bad for you, and it is too much work for her to make it for all of us. Wife " (between his mouth-fulls of pastry) "this is extra nice pie ; never tasted better" —which is a very masculine method of thanking you for letting him have his own way. For pie, substitute fruit for your own and children's dessert, and you will have the sweet satisfaction of thinking that if your children are brought up without pie, the wives of your sons will not be worn out with pie-making. But do not be so ungracious as to say this to or before your husband. The best way of making a dietetic reform general and radical is by bringing up the *children* on a healthful diet. If every mother and every person who has the care of children would give them only healthful food, they would not grow up with such vicious tastes as their parents have, and thus, in the course of time, the harmful dietetic habits of the nation would be eradicated. Again, John seeing his wife and children enjoying their fruit so much, will possibly—I may even say probably—be tempted to eat it himself. Almost all pies are filled with some kind of fruit, and he may like the latter in its natural state so well that he will prefer it without the pastry. And so, without any of those matrimonial disturbances and family jars which would have followed the wife's culinary refusal, the family will at last become a pieless one.

Few men care for cake. Most gentlemen consider it a rather effeminate food, and altogether too womanish for their masculine palates. So, if a wife takes upon herself the burden of making it, it is usually her own fault. But, for the sake of her own health and that of her children, let her substitute fruit.

The liking for hot white flour biscuits is about equally divided between men and women. The same remarks that I have made about a wife's duty to her husband and children concerning pie will apply with equal force to hot biscuit. But the best way to wean a man from them is to make delicious Graham bread. Sometimes a man is almost driven into eating hot biscuits by the inability of his wife to make good raised bread ; for it requires far less skill to make the former than the latter.

Sour bread has soured many a honeymoon, and many a husband's first cross word and many a bride's first tear have been caused by her inability to cook her "gude man" something fit to eat. To Vegetarianism, as a new and radical Cure for Intemperance, I earnestly invite the attention of our wives, mothers and daughters; for as it is in reality a question of diet, if the mistresses of the kitchen withhold their hearty co-operation, the whole thing will be a failure. The women of our land have done nobly in the great Temperance Reform of the past few years.

Hitherto their efforts have been directed to the hearts and minds of their erring brothers; now let them attend to their stomachs. Let the womanly tact, the love, the sympathy, the self-sacrifice, that have been so freely expended in moral and religious directions be turned into a dietetic channel, and if I mistake not, many poor inebriates, who have been considered hopelessly incurable will be saved and become useful and respected members of society.

Let this new method be adopted, not only in the drunkard's home, but in inebriate asylums. So far as my knowledge extends, it has never been tried in these institutions. It is to be sincerely wished that some enterprising person would establish an inebriate asylum on the Lax Vegetarian System. Let the drunkard's stomach and other parts that may be diseased receive therein the most approved and scientific treatment. Let special attention be given to the preparation of not only healthful but palatable and inviting food; for in this way the deprivation of meat will be less keenly felt.

Let "Mark Tapley" be a frequent visitor at the asylum, for "a merry heart doeth good like a medicine." Let the greatest love, tenderness and sympathy be shown to inebriates. Remember they are God's children, and however low they may have sunk in the social scale, do not despise them. I hope that all who may try this cure will carefully record their cases, and send them to the author, for it would give her the greatest pleasure to learn of the reformation of any poor unfortunate through her humble instrumentality.

HARRIET P. FOWLER.

Danvers, Mass.

THE END.

SEXUAL PHYSIOLOGY.

A SCIENTIFIC AND POPULAR EXPOSITION

OF THE

FUNDAMENTAL PROBLEMS IN SOCIOLOGY

BY R. T. TRALL, M.D

The great interest now being felt in all subjects relating to Human Development, will make the book OF INTEREST TO EVERY ONE. Besides the information obtained by its perusal, the practical bearing of the various subject. treated in improving and giving a higher direction and value to human life CAN NOT BE OVER-ESTIMATED.

This work contains the latest and most important discoveries in the Anatomy and Physiology of the Sexes; Explains the Origin of Human Life; How and when Menstruation, Impregnation, and Conception occur; giving the laws by which the number and sex of offspring are controlled, and valuable information in regard to the begetting and rearing of beautiful and healthy children. It is high-toned, and should be read by every family. With eighty fine engravings. *Agents wanted.*

This work has rapidly passed through ten editions, and the demand is constantly increasing. No such complete and valuable work has ever before been issued from the press. Price, by mail, $2.